The Last Manuscript

The Last Manuscript

Anurag Anurag

Contents

1

The Harrow Inheritance

The dense fog of early morning draped the streets of New York City in a gauzy veil, diffusing the reds and yellows of the traffic lights into a murky watercolor. On the 7:45 A.M. train to midtown, Eva Thompson stood swaying slightly with the motion of the car, her breath making little clouds on the window. The other passengers were absorbed in their phones, their books, a microcosm of the city's pulse.

Her stop arrived, and she stepped out onto the platform, the sounds of the city—the honking horns, the distant music of a street performer, the constant murmur of voices—greeting her like an old friend. Eva worked as an editor at Halloway Publishing, a prestigious but conservative house that often overlooked the potential of experimental writers. She had shoulder-length chestnut hair that caught the sun in glints of auburn and eyes that sparkled with a keen intellect, often hidden behind a pair of tortoiseshell glasses. Her attire was a careful balance of professional and bohemian, an expression of her dualistic nature.

Eva's phone rang with a sharpness that cut through the humdrum of the morning. The caller ID flashed 'Martin Adler', her boss. "Eva, you need to come to my office as soon as you get in," Martin's voice held a note of urgency she wasn't used to.

Upon entering the Halloway building, she noted the grandeur of the marble floors and the intricate woodwork on the walls that spoke of old New York's opulence. The leather-bound books on the receptionist's desk seemed to watch her as she passed.

Martin Adler's office was a spacious corner room with a view of the city that never failed to humble her. Martin, a stout man with an impressively groomed beard and glasses perpetually slipping down his nose, waved her in. The room smelled faintly of sandalwood and leather, a testament to his preference for the classics in both reading and interior design.

"Eva, I have some... unusual news," Martin began, handing her a manila envelope. "James Harrow left something for you."

Detective James Harrow, the legendary crime-solver turned crime-writer, had been a figure of fascination for Eva. His books were a blend of gritty reality and the complex moral quandaries of crime. Harrow had been a fan of adding humor in the grimmest situations—a quirk Eva appreciated.

Inside the envelope was a manuscript, 'The Last Case of James Harrow', and a note: 'To Eva, find the truth hidden within.'

Eva's heart raced. The manuscript felt like a relic of a bygone era, its edges worn, the title page emblazoned with Harrow's unmistakable scrawl. It was the beginning of a story, a challenge from beyond the grave.

She started reading right there, in Martin's office, and found herself laughing despite the gravity of the situation. Harrow's wit bled through the pages, lines like, "The suspect had an alibi as tight as a mall Santa's suit in December" reminding her why she admired him.

"Take the day, Eva. See what you can make of it," Martin said, with an uncharacteristically soft expression.

Her journey began with a visit to Harrow's old precinct. The building was an unimpressive brick structure, worn by the years and the weight of the stories it contained. Inside, she was greeted by the buzz of radios and the shuffling of papers, an orchestra of daily grind.

Detective Marcus Vale, Harrow's old partner, was a man weathered by the years like a sea cliff facing relentless waves. His eyes, a piercing blue, had a sharpness that seemed to take in more than possible, missing nothing. His handshake was firm, his smile quick to appear but slow to reach his eyes.

"Eva Thompson, the book editor. Harrow spoke highly of you," Marcus said, motioning her to a chair. "What can I do for you?"

They talked about Harrow—their cases, their disagreements, and even a few moments where Harrow's humor had cut the tension of a case like a knife through butter. Marcus reminisced with a chuckle, "One time, Harrow convinced the captain that the precinct cat was a confidential informant. Had him signing off on cans of tuna for 'information payments' for weeks."

The conversation took a turn when Eva mentioned the manuscript. Marcus's demeanor shifted, his eyes clouding over. "James was onto something, but it was making him paranoid. He wouldn't even trust me with the details."

As Eva left the precinct, the weather had taken a turn; the sky was now a steely gray, the wind picking up, rustling the paper in her hand as if eager to read Harrow's last words.

Eva's mind was a whirl of suspicions and possibilities as she made her way to a quaint café that Harrow used to frequent, a spot he'd described in one of his books as "the kind of place that could hide you from the world, or reveal you to it." The bell over the door jingled merrily in contrast to the gloom outside, and the smell of fresh pastries and strong coffee enveloped her.

A barista with a shock of pink hair and a nose ring glanced up from the espresso machine, a smile playing on her lips. "What can I get for you on this dreary day?"

"Something strong," Eva replied, returning the smile. "And maybe a little bit of local gossip on the side."

While waiting for her order, Eva took a seat by the window. The manuscript lay before her, its pages slightly damp from the rain. She couldn't help but thumb through them, drawn to Harrow's words like a detective to an unsolved case.

It was there that she met Lila Redding, Harrow's biographer. Lila was a tall woman, with an angular face that made her look severe until she smiled—a warm, disarming gesture that reached her intelligent green eyes. She carried herself with the assurance of someone who was used to asking difficult questions and expecting answers.

"Eva, darling, I heard about the manuscript," Lila said as she approached, her voice a smoky alto. "You know I have to see it."

They talked about Harrow, Lila painting a picture of a man whose humor was his armor and whose pen was his sword. The café around them was bustling, a cross-section of the city all within earshot of their conversation. Lila leaned in, lowering her voice, "James always said the truth is in the details. He'd hide things in plain sight, just for the keen observer."

"Like a message?" Eva asked, the intrigue deepening.

"Exactly. He loved riddles. Said they kept his mind sharp," Lila confided, sipping her coffee.

Outside, the rain began to patter against the window, casting reflective beads of light into the café's interior. It created an atmosphere that felt insulated from time, a capsule where secrets could be shared without reservation.

"Lila, did Harrow ever mention 'The Shadow' to you?" Eva queried, watching the other woman's face closely.

Lila's expression turned serious, her smile vanishing as quickly as it had appeared. "Only in whispers. It was his white whale, the case that got away. But he was onto something near the end. He said it was going to be his greatest reveal."

Eva's laughter from earlier was gone now, replaced by a solemn curiosity. She took a deep breath, feeling the weight of the task before her. Harrow's words had laid the foundation, but the building of the truth was hers to construct.

The rain intensified, streaking the windows and blurring the world outside. It seemed to Eva that the weather itself was trying to wash away the grime of the city, to clear a path for her to follow.

"You're going to pursue it, aren't you?" Lila asked, a note of admiration in her voice.

Eva nodded, her resolve hardening. "Harrow left me this manuscript for a reason. I'm going to find out why."

As the café door closed behind her, Eva felt the eyes of the patrons on her back, their murmurs a backdrop to her departure. She stepped out into the rain, the manuscript secure under her coat, and into the embrace of the city—with all its shadows and light, its secrets and revelations.

2

The Key and the Keeper

The evening was settling over New York City like a velvet shroud, the lights of the high rises twinkling against the encroaching darkness. Eva Thompson walked briskly down the sidewalk, her coat pulled tight against a sudden chill. Her mind was a whirlwind of clues, leads, and the haunting legacy of Detective James Harrow. The manuscript—a dense, cryptic document—was securely tucked under her arm, its contents promising revelations yet to be uncovered.

As she approached a small, dimly lit diner that seemed almost out of time with its neon sign flickering inconsistently, she decided it was the perfect place to ponder over the new information she'd gathered from her meeting with Marcus Vale and Lila Redding. The diner, with its old-fashioned booths and a jukebox playing soft jazz, offered a refuge from the harsh winds outside.

Eva slid into a booth near the back, away from the few scattered patrons who seemed engrossed in their own late-night solitudes. She ordered a coffee—black, no sugar—and laid the manuscript out on the table, her fingers brushing over the words James Harrow had typed. Her eyes were drawn to a margin note scribbled hastily, almost desperately, in Harrow's hand: "Follow the music."

Puzzled, she pondered the meaning. Harrow had been a detective with a knack for embedding deeper meanings in his work, but this seemed particularly cryptic. Was it literal music? Or something more metaphorical?

Her thoughts were interrupted by the arrival of her coffee and a slice of pie she hadn't ordered. The waitress, a middle-aged woman with a kind face and eyes that had seen much, smiled down at her. "On the house. You look like you could use a bit of sweetening up," she joked lightly.

Eva smiled gratefully, touched by the gesture, and as the waitress left, she took a moment to savor the warm, comforting aroma of the coffee. Then, diving back into the manuscript, she decided to decode Harrow's message.

As she read, a plan began to form. Harrow had often frequented a jazz club in his heyday, one that still operated not too far from where she was. Perhaps the reference to music was not so cryptic after all.

With a new destination in mind, she left the diner, the manuscript safe once more under her arm. The streets were slick with an earlier rain, reflecting the city lights in puddles like portals to another world. She made her way to the jazz club, its muted trumpet sign glowing in the darkness.

Inside, the atmosphere was thick with the soulful strains of a saxophone and the low murmur of an appreciative crowd. Eva made her way to the bar, ordered a drink, and looked around, letting the ambiance wash over her. It was here, in this melange of music and shadows, that she felt closest to understanding Harrow's mind.

She struck up a conversation with the bartender, a young man with an easy smile and a quick wit. "You ever hear of a guy named James Harrow?" she asked casually, not wanting to seem too eager.

The bartender's expression changed subtly. "Sure, he was a regular here. Always sat at the end of the bar, listening more to the people than the music, if you catch my drift."

Eva nodded, feeling a surge of excitement. "Did he ever meet anyone here? Someone unusual or memorable?"

"Yeah, there was this one guy—odd, kept to himself mostly, but Harrow talked to him a lot. They seemed... intense. Like they were both holding onto some big secret."

Eva's pulse quickened. This could be the lead she needed. She thanked the bartender, her mind racing with possibilities. Harrow had been onto something big, something that perhaps had led to his untimely death.

The night deepened around her as she left the club, the city's rhythms pulsing like a heartbeat beneath her feet. She knew what she had to do next.

Eva's next stop was "The Blue Moon," a jazz club that had managed to preserve its speakeasy aura despite the ever-changing cityscape around it. It was nestled on a narrow street where the neon signs flickered as if winking at passersby, tempting them with the secrets held within its walls.

As she pushed open the door, a wave of music rolled over her, a sultry saxophone solo weaving through the smoky air. The club was alive with the murmur of conversations, laughter tinkling like piano keys, glasses clinking in a rhythmic percussion. The patrons were an eclectic mix, from the besuited businessmen loosening their ties to the avant-garde artists whose clothes were as expressive as their art.

Finding a spot at the bar, she ordered a gin and tonic, her eyes scanning the room. The bartender, a man with the name tag 'Joe', had a face like leather, weathered and etched with lines of laughter and sorrow. His hands were steady as he mixed drinks, but his eyes missed nothing—a quality that reminded Eva of Harrow.

"You knew James Harrow?" Eva asked, leaning in to make herself heard over the bass line of the music.

Joe's smile flickered with a touch of sadness. "Knew him? He was like part of the furniture here. That stool at the end was his throne," he said, nodding towards the far corner of the bar. "Sad what happened to him."

Eva nodded, taking a sip of her drink. "He ever talk to anyone unusual?"

Joe chuckled, "In this place? Define unusual."

"Someone who might stand out, even here," Eva clarified, offering a smile to soften her probing.

"Well, there was this one guy—came in looking like he'd just stepped out of a noir film. Fedora, trench coat, the works. Always met with James in that corner. They'd talk, sometimes argue. It was intense."

"Do you remember anything about him? A name, perhaps?"

Joe shook his head, "No name, but he had a scar, right here," he pointed to his own cheek, "like a dueling scar. And he always paid in cash, old bills like you don't see much anymore."

Eva thanked him, her mind racing with this new information. A man out of time, meeting with Harrow, the intensity of their conversations—it was a clue she couldn't ignore.

Making her way to Harrow's 'throne,' she perched on the stool, trying to imagine the conversations that took place here. The music swelled, a haunting trumpet solo that seemed to speak directly to her, filling the spaces between her thoughts.

"First time here?" A voice cut through her reverie, smooth and curious.

She turned to see a man in his early thirties, his eyes bright with mischief. He wore a vest that didn't quite match his slacks, and a tie that looked like it had been knotted by someone with a vendetta against conformity.

"Is it that obvious?" Eva replied, her lips curving in amusement.

"A little," he admitted with a grin. "I'm Alex, by the way. Saxophonist.

And you're sitting in Harrow's seat. That makes you either brave or foolish."

"Eva. And maybe a bit of both," she said, extending her hand.

His handshake was firm, yet there was a gentleness to it. "You're here because of Harrow, aren't you? Trying to pick up where he left off?"

Eva raised an eyebrow, impressed by his perceptiveness. "What makes you say that?"

Alex tapped the side of his nose, "You've got that look—like you're searching for something that can't be found in the bottom of a glass."

Their conversation was interrupted by a sudden, harsh crackle from the speaker system, making several patrons flinch. A voice came on, dripping with sarcasm, "Ladies and gentlemen, please excuse the intrusion. We're experiencing technical difficulties, otherwise known as 'our sound guy tripped over the cord.' Normal service will resume shortly."

A collective chuckle rippled through the club as the music started up again. It was moments like this that cut through the tension, a shared joke among strangers in the night.

"I'll let you in on a secret," Alex said, leaning closer, his voice a conspiratorial whisper, "Harrow left something with the owner—a package or a letter, maybe. Said it was for safekeeping."

Eva's pulse quickened. This was the break she needed. "Do you think the owner would talk to me?"

Alex's smile was a flash in the dim light. "For James Harrow's protégé? I'm sure he'd make an exception."

She offered a grateful smile.

"Would you introduce me?" Eva inquired, her voice laced with a hopeful undertone.

"I'd be happy to introduce you," Alex said, finishing his drink. "But first, indulge my curiosity—what's a book editor doing playing detective?"

Eva leaned back, the leather of the booth creaking softly. "I guess I'm trying to figure out if the pen is mightier than the sword, or in this case, the murderer's weapon."

Alex let out a low chuckle, "Well, just make sure you don't end up on the wrong side of an epilogue."

Eva couldn't help but smile, "Noted."

The atmosphere of the club hummed with the buzz of the crowd, each table a small act in the larger play of the night. Eva was acutely aware of the stories unfolding around her, the drama, the intrigue, the whispered secrets.

Alex stood and offered her his hand, "Come on, let's go meet the keeper of Harrow's enigmatic legacy."

She followed him through the throng, their path lit by the soft glow of table lamps casting halos in the smoky air. They stopped in front of a door marked 'Private', Alex rapping a steady beat against the wood.

The door swung open to reveal a man in his fifties, his hair more salt than pepper, and a pair of reading glasses perched precariously on the bridge of his nose. He was dressed in an elegant waistcoat and tie, a stark contrast to the casual demeanor of his face.

"Alex, my boy, what brings you to my humble backstage?" the man inquired with a voice as smooth as the cognac he was known to favor.

"This is Eva," Alex introduced, "James Harrow left something in your care, and she's here to collect."

The man's gaze shifted to Eva, a flicker of recognition passing over his features. "Ah, the editor! I heard about you. Harrow said you had a mind like a steel trap."

Eva extended her hand, "Eva Thompson. You must be the owner, Mr...?"

"Just call me Clifford," he said, shaking her hand with a firm grip. "Come on in, let's talk."

They stepped into an office that was a shrine to the golden age of jazz, with vintage posters lining the walls and a gramophone that looked as though it could still spin a tune or two. Clifford motioned to a chair, taking a seat behind a desk cluttered with paperwork and memories.

"So, what's the deal with this mysterious package?" Eva asked, getting straight to the point.

Clifford leaned back, the chair groaning under the weight of untold stories. "Harrow was a man of many secrets. He left a package with me—a safety deposit box key, said if anything ever happened to him, I should wait for you or someone from his lineage."

Eva's curiosity peaked. "Do you have it with you?"

Clifford opened a drawer, rummaging through it before producing a small, brass key. He placed it on the desk, pushing it towards her. "It's yours now. Whatever's in there, he trusted you with it."

She picked up the key, feeling the cool metal against her skin, a tangible connection to Harrow and the mystery that surrounded his death. "Thank you, Clifford. You've been incredibly helpful."

As she stood to leave, Clifford added, "Harrow was a good man, caught up in a dangerous game. Be careful, Ms. Thompson. Not all stories have a happy ending."

Eva nodded solemnly, "I'll remember that."

Walking down the street, her shadow stretched long behind her, a silent companion in the quest for the truth. The city, with its cacophony of life, seemed to whisper Harrow's name with every step she took. And Eva Thompson was listening.

3

Signals in the Static

New York greeted the dawn with a grudging acceptance, the skyline a series of silhouettes against a lightening sky. Eva Thompson made her way to the bank on Fifth Avenue, the brass key from Clifford burning a hole in her pocket. The streets were already pulsing with the city's relentless energy, cabs honking and street vendors setting up for the day.

The bank was an edifice of old wealth, its marble floors echoing with the click of Eva's heels. She approached the safety deposit box area, where a young man with meticulously styled hair and a suit that screamed 'I have a personal tailor' greeted her.

"Good morning, welcome to Manhattan Trust. How may I assist you?" he asked with a rehearsed charm that didn't quite reach his eyes.

"I need to access a safety deposit box. I have a key," Eva said, presenting the brass key to him.

The clerk examined the key, his brow raising slightly. "Very well, Ms...?"

"Thompson, Eva Thompson."

He led her through a series of secured doors to a room lined with safety deposit boxes. The clerk pointed her to the correct one. "Is there anything else you need, Ms. Thompson?"

Eva shook her head, "I should be fine, thank you."

Left alone, she inserted the key and the lock clicked open. Inside the box was a small, brown envelope, worn at the edges as if it had been handled repeatedly. Eva carefully opened it to find a series of photographs and a USB drive. The photographs were of various scenes around the city, each marked with a date and time, but no further explanation.

Intrigued, Eva pocketed the USB drive and the photos and made her way out of the bank, the clerk giving her a nod that managed to be both courteous and dismissive.

Outside, the city had fully awakened, the sun casting a harsh light on the skyscrapers. Eva decided to head to her office at Halloway Publishing to examine the contents of the drive. The lobby of the building was bustling with the morning rush, editors and writers buzzing around like bees in a hive.

Her colleague, Michael, approached her, a stack of manuscripts in his arms. He was a man who could only be described as 'rumpled', with hair that always looked in need of a comb and a tie perpetually askew.

"Eva, heard you took a personal day yesterday. Digging up dirt on your mystery author?" Michael asked, a teasing glint in his eye.

Eva rolled her eyes, "Something like that."

She made her way to her office, a small room with a view of the alley, the fire escape casting shadows that danced with the breeze. She inserted the USB drive into her computer, and a series of audio files appeared, each labeled with the same dates and times as the photos.

Pressing play on the first file, Eva was greeted with the ambient sounds of the city, but as she listened more closely, other layers emerged—muffled conversations, the distant wail of sirens, a dog barking. She listened to each file in turn, trying to discern a pattern, a clue to their significance.

As the day bled into evening, she sat back in frustration. She was missing something, a link to make sense of Harrow's audio montage. A knock on her office door broke her concentration.

Standing in the doorway was her intern, Jenny, a bright-eyed journalism major with a penchant for speaking in hashtags and an optimism that Eva found both endearing and exhausting.

"#DisturbanceAlert. You've been holed up here all day. Thought you might need sustenance," Jenny said, holding out a cup of coffee and a bagel.

Eva accepted with a grateful smile. "Thanks, Jenny. I'm just going over some... research."

"Anything I can help with?" Jenny asked, peeking at the screen with curiosity.

"Unless you can tell me what a series of random city sounds have to do with a cold case, I'm afraid not."

Jenny's eyes sparkled with challenge. "Never underestimate the power of a fresh pair of ears. Play it again?"

Eva shrugged and hit play. As the sounds filled the room again, Jenny closed her eyes, listening intently.

"Wait, go back to 02:15 on the third file. There! Do you hear that? The sequence of beeps—it's like a coded message or something."

Eva replayed the segment, a series of high-pitched tones rising above the city's drone. It was a pattern, deliberate and rhythmic.

"You're a genius, Jenny!" Eva exclaimed.

Jenny grinned, "#AudioDetective."

Eva chuckled, her fatigue momentarily forgotten. "Let's see if we can crack this code. It's just the breakthrough we needed."

Eva and Jenny hunched over the computer, their heads almost touching as they replayed the sequence of beeps. The small office felt cozier with the companionship, the early evening light casting a warm glow through the blinds.

"You know, if we figure this out, I'm totally getting this story published. #BreakingNews," Jenny said with a wink.

"Let's not get ahead of ourselves," Eva replied, though she couldn't help smiling at Jenny's enthusiasm.

The pattern was a sequence of seven distinct tones, repeating several times. Eva tapped her fingers on the desk, counting the intervals. "It's Morse code," she declared, a spark of excitement in her voice.

"Morse what-now?" Jenny quipped, her brow furrowed.

Eva chuckled. "Morse code, it's an old form of communication using sounds or lights. It's how people sent messages before the days of #Hashtags and DMs."

With a quick search, they pulled up a Morse code chart. Together, they translated the beeps: D-A-N-G-E-R-S-T-O-P.

The room suddenly felt colder, the playful atmosphere evaporating. "That's... ominous," Jenny said, her tone serious for once.

Eva nodded, her mind racing. Harrow had known he was in danger and had left a breadcrumb trail for someone he trusted to follow.

Just then, the door burst open and in waltzed Martin Adler, the publisher at Halloway, his personality filling the room before he even spoke. He was a man whose flamboyant ties were only outshone by his booming voice.

"Eva, my star editor! Why the long face? We should be celebrating!" Martin boomed, clapping his hands together.

Eva raised an eyebrow, "Celebrating what, exactly?"

"Why, the latest sales reports, of course! Our true crime section is through the roof, all thanks to you and your golden touch."

Martin's joviality was infectious, but Eva couldn't shake off the chill from the message. "That's great, Martin, but I think I've stumbled upon something big here."

Martin's expression shifted from mirth to interest. "Oh? Do tell."

Eva explained the sequence of events, from the manuscript to the safety deposit box, and finally, the Morse code message. Martin listened intently, nodding along.

When she finished, Martin stroked his chin, his eyes alight. "This is the stuff of novels, Eva! If you solve this, you're writing the book, and I'm publishing it!"

Jenny clapped her hands, "#Bestseller!"

The mood lightened once again, and even Eva had to admit there was a thrill to the idea. "First, we need to figure out what Harrow was warning us about," she said, determination edging her voice.

The trio stood together, united by the mystery that lay before them. The last rays of sunlight dipped below the horizon, and the office took on the hush of twilight. The day's end was just the beginning of their investigation.

With a new clue and a team formed by chance and curiosity, Eva set her sights on unraveling the truth. Harrow's last message was a siren call, and she would follow it to the end, come what may. The night beckoned, and with it, the promise of answers hidden in the cacophony of the city's melody.

Harmonies of the Hidden

Under the cloak of an indigo twilight, the city's architecture became silhouettes against a watercolor sky. Eva stood on the rooftop of her apartment building, the Manhattan skyline sprawling before her—a forest of concrete and glass. She took a deep breath, the air crisp with the scent of impending rain.

The Morse code, 'DANGER STOP', echoed in her mind, a haunting refrain that suggested the manuscript held darker secrets than she had initially thought. She turned to Jenny, who had accompanied her to this quiet refuge above the city's chaos.

"So, Morse code," Jenny said, breaking the silence. "That's like old-school texting, right?"

Eva smiled, appreciating Jenny's attempt to lighten the mood. "Very old-school. But the question is, what was Harrow trying to communicate, and to whom?"

As they discussed the possibilities, the door to the rooftop creaked open, and out stepped Michael, Halloway's in-house true crime expert. His hair was more disheveled than usual, as if he had run his hands through it all day. In his hand was the manuscript, its pages now dog-eared from use

.

"Figured you'd be up here," Michael said, joining them. "I've been through this manuscript front to back, and the way Harrow talks about 'The Shadow'... It's personal, almost obsessive."

Eva took the manuscript from him, flipping through the pages. "He was closing in on something—or someone."

The air grew heavy with the threat of rain, and a distant rumble of thunder added a dramatic underscore to their conversation. The first few raindrops began to fall, speckling the manuscript's pages.

"Let's head inside before this becomes 'The Last Drenched Manu-script'," Michael quipped, leading the way back to the warmth of Eva's apartment.

Once inside, surrounded by the eclectic mix of modern and vintage decor, they spread the photographs from the safety deposit box across the coffee table. The images were a scattered puzzle, each depicting a different location in the city, always at night.

Eva picked up a photo of a dilapidated pier. "Look at this," she pointed to a figure in the background, barely discernible. "Could that be 'The Shadow'?"

Michael leaned in, squinting at the figure. "Or it could be a fisherman."

Jenny snorted. "Yeah, because fishermen love to hang out at creepy piers at night."

The mood was a blend of tension and camaraderie, the gravity of their task tinged with the humor that came from their growing familiarity.

Eva inserted the USB drive into her laptop, the hum of the machine cutting through the silence. The sound files played, filling the room with the cacophony of city life, each one a piece of Harrow's auditory diary.

The thunderstorm outside crescendoed, a symphony that mingled with the urban soundtrack emanating from the speakers.

"Wait," Eva said suddenly, pausing the third file. "This sound here— it's not just background noise. It's the same series of tones as the Morse code, but it's part of the ambient sound. Harrow was documenting something he heard repeatedly."

Michael rubbed his chin, a flash of insight crossing his face. "And if it's a sound that's part of the cityscape, it might be a clue to a specific location. We need to pinpoint where this was recorded."

Jenny jumped up, her youthful energy infectious. "Road trip! Or, well, creepy night-time city exploration trip!"

They shared a laugh, the absurdity of their amateur sleuthing not lost on them. But beneath the laughter was a shared determination, a need to solve the puzzle Harrow had left behind.

Armed with the photographs, the manuscript, and the audio files, the trio prepared to delve into the depths of the city. They would chase the phantom notes through the concrete jungle, seeking the conductor of this deadly orchestra.

Eva felt the weight of responsibility, the importance of continuing Harrow's legacy. The last manuscript was more than a title; it was a testament to a life's work, and she was the custodian of its final chapter.

Under the lambent glow of the city that never sleeps, the torrential downpour had turned the streets into a reflective tapestry of neon and streetlights. Eva, Jenny, and Michael, armed with the clues left by Harrow, ventured into the heart of the metropolis, determined to chase down the phantom sounds that could lead them to 'The Shadow'.

They found themselves outside an all-night diner whose neon sign flickered intermittently, the 'N' sputtering out every few seconds. The scent of grease and coffee mingled with the petrichor of the rain-soaked streets.

"Remember, we're looking for anything that matches the sounds from the audio files. It could be anything, a signal, a particular horn... anything," Eva instructed, her voice firm over the sound of the rain tapping against her umbrella.

Michael nodded, pushing his wet hair out of his eyes. "I feel like I'm in one of those old detective movies, except my feet are wet, and I forgot to charge my phone."

Jenny laughed, punching his arm playfully. "C'mon, Detective Downer, let's crack this case so we can all get dry."

The first location was an intersection teeming with life, even in the wee hours. A food vendor was packing up for the night, the clatter of his cart rhythmic and metallic. Eva listened closely, then shook her head. "Not here."

As they moved through the city, they reached a bridge, the river below churning with the evening's storm. The sound of a foghorn cut through the air, long and low. Eva paused, signaling them to stop.

"This could be it. Harrow mentioned the river in his manuscript," she said, her voice barely audible above the rumble of the traffic.

Jenny shivered, hugging her arms. "I hope 'The Shadow' appreciates us getting drenched for the sake of his capture."

They recorded the foghorn, comparing it to the tones on Eva's phone. It was a match—the pattern was unmistakable.

A shadow loomed over them, and they spun around to see a figure under a large umbrella. A police badge glinted under the streetlight as the figure approached.

"Detective Marcus Vale, at your service," the newcomer announced, a wry smile on his face. "I see Harrow's manuscript has turned you into night owls."

Vale was a rugged veteran with eyes that seemed to have witnessed the spectrum of human behavior. His coat, a few sizes too big, made him look like a bear on two legs.

"You following us, detective, or is this a serendipitous meeting in the rain?" Eva asked, her tone equal parts suspicious and welcoming.

"Bit of both. Harrow was a friend, and I have a vested interest in seeing this through," Vale replied, his voice carrying the weight of unsaid stories.

Eva considered him for a moment before nodding. "Then you're welcome to join our... what did you call it, Jenny? Our 'creepy night-time city exploration trip'?"

Jenny giggled, offering Vale a high-five. "Welcome to the club, Detective Bear."

Together, they stood on the bridge, the cityscape a canvas of light and shadow around them. The rain began to ease, the foghorn's call a beacon in the night leading them to the next piece of the puzzle.

"So, what's next?" Vale asked, his demeanor shifting to one of readiness.

Eva held up the photograph of the pier. "We follow the river down to Pier 39. If we're right, that's where Harrow heard this horn, where he saw something—or someone—important."

The group set off, the city's relentless rhythm underscored by the pulsing question in their hearts: What was Harrow trying to tell them? With each step, they wove through the narrative Harrow had left behind, their own stories entangling with his, a tapestry of past and present mysteries.

And somewhere in the distance, 'The Shadow' waited, a dark author of unsolved chapters, unaware that his audience was drawing ever closer.

5

The Echoes of Pier 39

The dampness of the night was beginning to retreat as Eva, Jenny,

Michael, and Detective Vale approached Pier 39. The wooden planks groaned under their feet, a chorus accompanied by the slosh of the Hudson's waves. A fog, thin and wispy, clung to the water's surface, and the distant glow of the city bled into the sky, fighting back the dark.

Eva paused, a hand raised for silence. "This is the spot from the photo," she said, pointing to a rusted sign partially obscured by the fog.

"Creepy and secluded, Harrow had a flair for the dramatic," Michael quipped, pulling his coat tighter around him.

Jenny, ever the social media maven, snapped a photo. "#MysteryPier," she whispered, a smile tugging at her lips despite the seriousness of their task.

Detective Vale was examining the surroundings, his gaze sharp. "If Harrow came here, it was for a reason. Look for anything out of place."

They split up, their footsteps echoing in the quiet. The sound of the city was a distant hum, the clamor of the day's beginning held at bay by the water's expanse.

Eva's attention was caught by an odd shape near the edge of the pier. She crouched down, brushing away the detritus of the tide to reveal a weather-beaten notebook. She carefully opened it, the pages swollen with moisture, the ink smeared. "Guys, over here!"

Jenny and Michael rushed over, while Vale approached with measured steps. "What did you find?" Vale asked, peering over her shoulder.

"It's a logbook, or it was. It's mostly ruined, but look here," Eva pointed to a page, the handwriting still legible. "It's a list of dates and times, and look, the initials 'T.S.' It has to be 'The Shadow'."

Michael scratched his head, "Or 'Tantalizing Soup'. Could Harrow have been a secret food critic?"

Jenny rolled her eyes but laughed. "Sure, and these are all the times he was disappointed by the clam chowder."

Vale's chuckle was a deep rumble, like distant thunder. "You two should take this act on the road."

A shout from the far end of the pier drew their attention. They found a security guard, his uniform slightly too small, making him look as if he'd been poured into it. He was standing next to an unassuming door half-hidden by shadows.

"Can I help you folks? This pier's not safe at night," he called out, not unkindly.

"We're just looking into something for a friend," Eva explained as they approached him.

The guard eyed them with a mix of curiosity and skepticism. "Your friend wouldn't happen to be Detective Harrow, would it?"

"You knew him?" Vale asked, stepping forward.

"Knew of him. He'd come here some nights, just staring out at the water. Said it helped him think. I figured he was just another city soul searching for answers in the waves," the guard shared.

"Did you ever see him meet anyone here?" Eva inquired, her voice steady.

"Nah, he was always alone. Though he did ask me about the old ferry terminal once, wanted to know when it shut down."

Jenny, unable to resist, quipped, "Did he have a thing for abandoned places, or was it the ghosts he was after?"

"Ghosts don't scare me. It's the living you've got to worry about," the guard replied, though his smirk suggested he appreciated Jenny's humor.

Eva thanked the guard, and they stepped away, huddling to discuss their next move.

"An abandoned ferry terminal," Vale mused. "That could be our next stop."

"More dark, spooky places? Harrow really knew how to pick 'em," Michael said, his tone light to mask his unease.

Eva was already moving, the notebook clutched in her hand. "Let's go ghost hunting, then."

As they left the pier, the city began to stir more insistently, the pulse of the imminent morning creeping into their bones.

Their small group trod along the cobbled streets, the old ferry terminal looming ahead like a sentinel. Its once-bustling docks were now silent, the air heavy with the tang of brine and rust. The terminal was a skeleton of its former self, with empty windows staring out like hollow eye sockets.

"This is like a scene straight out of a horror movie," Jenny remarked, half expecting an orchestra to start playing suspenseful music.

Michael nudged her, "If you hear a violin, start running."

The terminal gate was chained, but years of neglect had left a gap just wide enough for them to slip through. The ground was littered with debris, and the once bright paint on the walls was peeling away like aged skin.

Detective Vale's flashlight cut through the darkness, casting eerie shadows on the walls. "Watch your step," he warned, as his light revealed the splintered remains of an old ticket booth.

As they ventured further, the beam of Vale's light landed on a mural, its colors faded but the image still discernible—a ferry cutting through the waves under a moonlit sky. "Looks like Harrow wasn't the only one who found inspiration here," Vale commented.

Eva ran her fingers over the mural, her touch gentle. "He was drawn to places like this, full of stories and secrets."

A sudden noise startled them, a skittering sound in the dark. Michael's yelp was loud in the quiet, and when the beam of the flashlight revealed a rat darting away, Jenny couldn't suppress her laughter. "Your scream is the scariest thing here, Michael."

Michael huffed, trying to regain his composure. "I have a very healthy respect for rabies, thank you very much."

Their search brought them to an old office, the door ajar. Inside, the air was musty, filled with the ghosts of old timetables and ticket stubs. A desk stood in the center, a single drawer slightly open.

Vale motioned for Eva to open it. Inside, they found a collection of tapes, each labeled with a date and the same initials, 'T.S.'

Eva's breath caught. "This could be what we're looking for. These dates correspond to the logbook we found."

The tapes felt like a time capsule, a direct line to the past Harrow had been chasing. "We need to listen to these," Eva said, her voice a mix of anticipation and dread.

Michael leaned against the desk, a smirk playing on his lips despite the gravity of their find. "Great, who's got a tape player? Anyone?"

Jenny rolled her eyes, "We'll find one, Detective Antiquities."

They gathered the tapes, the potential answers they held making the terminal seem less desolate, less abandoned. It was a repository of whispers waiting to be heard.

As they left the terminal, the first light of dawn was creeping into the sky, the city awakening around them. The night had been long, and the rain had finally ceased, leaving the world fresh and new.

Eva looked back at the terminal, its silhouette softened by the morning light. The last manuscript was not just a collection of pages; it was a map, guiding them through the hidden alleys of truth and the shadowed corners of justice.

They stepped out from the embrace of the terminal, the echoes of the past trailing behind them, a symphony of history's secrets ready to be revealed.

6

❧

A Tape in Time

The vintage electronics store 'Halcyon Days' was a cavern of treasures, a trove where past technologies found their afterlife. Eva, Jenny, Michael, and Detective Vale stepped inside from the emerging daylight, their senses immediately overwhelmed by the musk of aging circuitry and the patina of bygone eras that clung to every surface.

As Sal, the proprietor, ushered them towards a stout, dust-covered reel-to-reel tape player, Michael couldn't help but quip, "So this is where gadgets come to retire. Do they get a pension too?"

Sal, a grizzled man with hands like leather maps and eyes that twinkled with the wisdom of years, let out a laugh that rumbled from his chest.

"Only the satisfaction of a job well done," he retorted, his deft fingers threading the tape with practiced ease.

The group gathered around the machine as it hummed to life, the reels beginning to turn. The soft hiss of the tape was like a time machine, drawing them back to the days of Harrow's investigation.

Eva leaned in as the first sounds spilled into the shop, "Listen for anything that stands out, anything that Harrow might have heard that led him to 'The Shadow'."

As Harrow's recorded voice filled the room, recounting shadowed figures and close calls, Jenny couldn't suppress a shiver. "It's like he's here with us... kind of spooky if you ask me."

Vale, arms crossed, nodded solemnly. "Harrow was good, one of the best. If he left these tapes, they're the key to cracking this case wide open."

Through the crackle and pop of the audio, a pattern emerged. Street noises, code sequences, and fragments of a larger puzzle began to take shape. It was a sonic blueprint to 'The Shadow's' haunts and habits.

Sal, now leaning against a shelf lined with radios that had seen better decades, wiped his hands on his apron. "Seems like you've got quite the mystery on your hands. This fella, 'The Shadow', some sort of ghost?"

"More like a phantom hiding behind a veil of power and fear," Eva said, her gaze not leaving the tape player.

The reels stopped, and they were left in the silence of the shop, the weight of Harrow's last investigation hanging heavily in the air.

"So, where to now?" Michael asked, breaking the quiet. "We've got sounds and sights, times and dates... but what's our next step?"

Jenny, ever the optimist, chimed in, "We hit the streets. Follow in Harrow's footsteps, see the city through his eyes... and ears."

Eva collected the tapes, her resolve hardening. "We retrace Harrow's last days, visit the places he mentioned here. Somewhere out there, amidst the hustle of the city, is the clue that will lead us to 'The Shadow'."

Vale nodded, "Let's get moving. Time's not our ally."

They thanked Sal, stepping out of the timewarped confines of 'Halcyon Days' into the modern rush of the city, a stark contrast to the nostalgia they'd left behind. The streets were beginning to fill, the city's pulse quickening as the morning progressed.

As they moved through the waking city, a plan began to take shape. They would visit each location Harrow had surveilled, listening to the corresponding tape, searching for the auditory clue that would lead them to the truth.

It was a race against time and shadows, with only the echoes of the past to guide them. But with each step, they drew closer to unmasking 'The Shadow', and each heartbeat brought them nearer to the crescendo of Harrow's final symphony.

7

∽

The Cipher of Silence

The morning bustle of New York City formed a chaotic backdrop as Eva, Jenny, Michael, and Detective Vale sequestered themselves in the back room of a quiet, hole-in-the-wall coffee shop. The walls were lined with local art, and the air was a tapestry woven from the scent of roasted coffee beans and the faint hint of paint and varnish. Outside, the weather was a typical city daybreak—hazy sunlight with the promise of a clear afternoon.

Vale spread out the tapes and the manuscript on an aged oak table, its surface scarred with the memories of countless cups and elbows. "If Harrow didn't go to the authorities with this, there must've been a damn good reason."

Eva picked up one of the tapes, turning it over in her hand. "These tapes, the manuscript, the Morse code... They're pieces of a larger puzzle. Harrow was meticulous. He wouldn't have left anything to chance."

Michael, flipping through the manuscript, frowned. "You think he was afraid of something? Or someone? This all reads like a man trying to outsmart a ghost."

Jenny sipped her latte, a smirk playing on her lips despite the gravity of the situation. "More like outsmarting a poltergeist with connections in high places."

Vale's brow creased as he pondered their words. "I've been around long enough to know that some ghosts have the power to reach beyond the grave. If 'The Shadow' is who I think it is, Harrow knew that taking him down meant playing the long game."

Eva nodded, the pieces starting to come together. "The manuscript's last chapter—what if it's not just Harrow's concluding remarks? What if it's a coded message to lead us to where 'The Shadow' can be found, and more importantly, to where Harrow left evidence he knew couldn't be ignored?"

The group leaned in, the manuscript suddenly more than just words on a page. It was Harrow's final gambit.

As they dissected the text, line by line, a pattern emerged. The narrative was punctuated with odd phrasings, peculiar word choices. Eva began to jot down notes, her mind racing.

Michael let out a low whistle. "You're saying Harrow hid a cipher in his last chapter? This reads like something out of a spy novel."

"And the Morse code?" Jenny asked, eyebrows raised. "How does that fit into all this?"

"It's a time stamp," Vale said, a light of realization in his eyes. "Each sequence in the Morse code corresponds to a time Harrow witnessed something crucial. Something that could incriminate 'The Shadow'."

The coffee shop owner, a stout man with an accent as thick as the espresso he brewed, leaned over their table, curiosity piqued by their intense discussion. "You folks working on a movie script? Because if you need a location, my cousin has this old warehouse by the docks. Very scenic."

They shared a brief, nervous chuckle, the suggestion breaking the tension for a moment. "Something like that," Eva replied, her smile not quite reaching her eyes.

Jenny nudged Michael. "Hey, we might take you up on that. Who knows where this story will lead us?"

With a fresh pot of coffee courtesy of the intrigued owner, they dove back into Harrow's cryptic clues. Outside, the city carried on, unaware that within the walls of this unassuming shop, four individuals were on the brink of exposing a truth that would shake the very foundations of their world.

The manuscript, the Morse code, the tapes—they were all conduits to a revelation that Harrow had sacrificed everything to make known. Now, it was up to Eva and her team to ensure his sacrifices were not in vain.

As they poured over Harrow's cryptic last chapter, the cozy confines of the coffee shop felt like a world apart from the clamor of New York City waking up. The barista, a tall man with an ironic mustache and a tattoo sleeve of mythical creatures, was polishing glasses behind the counter, casting occasional curious glances at the group's intense discussion.

Eva was the first to break the silence after the store owner's departure. "Harrow knew the risks of going public without solid proof. He was out-maneuvered but not outplayed. These tapes and the manuscript... they're breadcrumbs."

Jenny piped up, "Breadcrumbs leading to a big bad wolf, or in this case, a shadow with teeth."

Vale, studying the tapes, added, "We're not dealing with a run-of-the-mill criminal. 'The Shadow' is connected, protected."

Michael, while examining the manuscript, let out a frustrated sigh. "So Harrow lays out a path in his narrative, a path veiled in allegory and metaphor, only clear to those who know how to read it."

"Exactly," Eva said, her fingers tracing the lines of text. "He's describing locations, events, but it's all under the guise of a fiction narrative. We need to decode the allegory to find the real-world counterparts."

A new voice chimed in, deep and smooth, with an edge of authority. They turned to see a man in a neatly pressed suit standing by their table.

His badge identified him as Captain Jonathan Reid of the NYPD, his eyes sharp and assessing.

"Detective Vale, I see you've pulled together quite the investigative team," Reid observed, his gaze lingering on each of them.

Vale stood up, a hand extended. "Captain Reid, meet the team that's about to crack the Harrow case wide open."
Eva introduced herself and the others, their focus shifting to include the new arrival.

Reid nodded, his expression unreadable. "I've been following your progress. Harrow was a friend. I want to see this through, but I warn you, the waters you're navigating are murkier than the Hudson."

Jenny couldn't help but murmur, "And probably twice as polluted."

Reid cracked a smile, a brief show of camaraderie. "Exactly. 'The Shadow' is no ordinary criminal. He's someone with the power to evade the law, to hide in plain sight."

Eva leaned forward, her gaze intense. "We believe Harrow left a message, something that would lead us to conclusive evidence."

"The kind of evidence that could cast a light on the darkest corners," Michael added, eager to demonstrate their progress.

Reid's demeanor suggested he was weighing the risks, calculating the next move in a high-stakes game of chess. "Be careful," he cautioned. "In my experience, those who lurk in the shadows are adept at extinguishing lights that get too close."

With a final nod, Reid left as quietly as he had appeared, leaving them with a renewed sense of the dangers ahead.

As they resumed their work, the coffee shop became their command center. The barista brought over refills, his curiosity piqued. "You guys are like a real-life detective novel. Need an extra character?"

Michael laughed, accepting the coffee. "Thanks, but I think we have our hands full with the cast we've got."

Jenny peered at the manuscript, tapping a line with her finger. "What if these locations aren't just settings for Harrow's stories, but places where he's stashed evidence?"

Vale nodded, the pieces clicking into place. "Then we need to map out these allegories, find the true landmarks he's pointing us towards."

They worked methodically, dissecting Harrow's prose, uncovering the layers of meaning woven through the narrative. The manuscript became not just a book, but a guide, each chapter a veiled directive leading them deeper into the heart of the mystery.

Outside, the city was in full swing, the energy palpable even within the coffee shop's walls. But inside, time stood still as Eva and her team unraveled the enigma Harrow had left behind, each revelation bringing them closer to a showdown with 'The Shadow'.

And as the day progressed, the humor that peppered their conversation became the light that kept the looming darkness at bay. They were no longer just individuals brought together by chance and circumstance; they were a team, united in purpose and resolve, ready to face whatever lay ahead.

8

Echoes and Alibis

In the bustling heart of Midtown, amidst the cacophony of honking taxis and chattering crowds, Eva, Jenny, Michael, and Detective Vale settled into the relative calm of an old map room in the public library. The ornate ceiling loomed high above, adorned with frescoes that told tales of exploration and discovery—a fitting canopy for their quest.

"Okay, so each of these tapes corresponds to a location Harrow staked out," Eva stated, unrolling a large city map across the wooden table, its surface worn smooth by decades of scholarly elbows.

Jenny, with her hair tied back and a focused frown, pointed to a cluster of marks they had added to the map. "We've got the sites, the sounds... but what ties them together?"

As they debated, a library assistant approached, her steps soft against the marble floor. She was a petite woman, her hair the silver-gray of well-read pages, her glasses perched precariously on the bridge of her nose.

"Excuse me, I couldn't help overhearing. You're tracking historical locations? Might I suggest cross-referencing with the city archives?" she offered, her voice a whisper honed by years of library service.

"Thank you, we might just do that," Vale replied, tipping an imaginary hat. "You wouldn't happen to have a tape player as well, would you?"

With a knowing smile, she nodded. "Follow me, detectives of history."

They trailed behind her to a room that smelled of dust and ink. Here, nestled between shelves laden with records, was a tape player, its buttons worn from use.

Eva inserted the first tape and pressed play. Harrow's voice filled the space, a spectral presence among the archives. They listened, pausing the playback occasionally to debate a sound or a reference.

"Did you hear that?" Michael interrupted, rewinding the tape. "That siren in the background—it's old, like from the forties or fifties. They don't make that sound anymore."

Eva's eyes lit up. "Of course! Harrow was telling us when. These tapes aren't just where, they're when. He's pinpointing an event in time."

The library assistant beamed, pleased with her part in their deduction. "I do enjoy a good mystery. Be sure to let me know how this chapter ends."

As they matched dates to the historical records, a timeline began to form—a series of incidents, long forgotten by the city, but all too relevant to their investigation.

"Guys, look at this!" Jenny exclaimed, pointing to an old newspaper clipping. "A heist from the fifties, unsolved. The description of the suspect... it matches 'The Shadow's' M.O."

Vale leaned over her shoulder, his face serious. "He's been operating for decades. Harrow must've uncovered his identity, but needed irrefutable proof."

"The kind of proof that you don't take to the cops because you don't know who's in on it," Michael muttered.

Eva gathered the tapes. "We need to go to these locations, find what Harrow left behind. It's the only way to bring 'The Shadow' into the light."

They packed up their clues, the library's silence a stark contrast to the urgency of their mission. As they stepped back into the sunlight, the city greeted them with the chaos of midday, indifferent to the drama unfolding in its midst.

Their next stop was a historical building in Lower Manhattan. Its facade was a patchwork of repair and neglect, the ghosts of the city's past etched into its very bricks.

Here, they found the echo of the siren from the tape, a hidden compartment that held another piece of the puzzle—a photograph, decades old, depicting a man shaking hands with a city official. The man's face was obscured, but the handshake spoke of deals and power.

"That's our connection," Vale said grimly. "'The Shadow' isn't just a criminal; he's part of the city's fabric. Harrow knew exposing him would shake the city to its core."

As they continued their journey from one historical site to the next, the city seemed to watch, its skyscrapers like sentinels over their progress. Each location held a key, each key unlocked a secret, and with each secret, the silhouette of 'The Shadow' grew ever more defined.

By the time the sun began to dip toward the horizon, painting the sky in hues of fire and gold, they had amassed enough evidence to piece together a story of corruption and silence that had haunted the city for generations.

As the day closed, they knew what lay ahead. Confrontation, revelation, and the risk that comes with dragging shadows into the unforgiving light of truth. But together, they had become the bearers of Harrow's legacy, the tellers of the final chapter of a story.

They convened again at the coffee shop as dusk embraced the city. With the map unfurled amongst the remnants of their day's work, the connection was clear as the twilight outside.

"We've been chasing a chameleon," Vale said, the lines on his face deepening. "Someone who changes colors with the political landscape."

Eva nodded, the last pieces falling into place. "Harrow's clues weren't just about places and times; they were about power and the fear it wields."

Michael sipped his coffee, now cold. "You know, Harrow was kind of like a composer, and 'The Shadow' his reluctant muse."

Jenny, tapping her fingers on the table in thought, added, "Except this muse doesn't inspire beauty. He inspires bullet points in a case file."

The air in the shop was thick with the scent of espresso and the tension of their impending resolution. The patrons around them were oblivious to the drama, engrossed in their laptops and lattes.

Eva collected the photos and the tapes, her eyes meeting each of her companions in turn. "Tomorrow, we bring this to a close. We'll meet 'The Shadow' on our terms, with the evidence Harrow left us."

As they stepped out into the evening, the city's cacophony resumed, a reminder that life went on, indifferent to the justice being sought in its shadows. The neon lights of the shop flickered behind them, a silent salute to their quest.

"Anyone else feel like we're walking into a storm?" Michael asked, his humor a cloak for his nerves.

Jenny chuckled. "With this crew? It's more like we're the storm."

Vale gave a rare smile, glancing at the sky, which was clear for now. "Let's just hope 'The Shadow' is ready for the downpour."

Their path had been set by a symphony of clues, a composition of whispers and codes, and now, the final note awaited them. It was time to turn the page on 'The Shadow' and finish the story that James Harrow had been unable to complete.

In the symphony of the city, their footsteps were the rhythm, their resolve the melody, and the night ahead, the crescendo that would either be their triumph or their epilogue.

9

Unmasking the Silhouette

In the bustling heart of Midtown, amidst the cacophony of honking taxis and chattering crowds, Eva, Jenny, Michael, and Detective Vale settled into the relative calm of an old map room in the public library. The ornate ceiling loomed high above, adorned with frescoes that told tales of exploration and discovery—a fitting canopy for their quest.

"Okay, so each of these tapes corresponds to a location Harrow staked out," Eva stated, unrolling a large city map across the wooden table, its surface worn smooth by decades of scholarly elbows.

Jenny, with her hair tied back and a focused frown, pointed to a cluster of marks they had added to the map. "We've got the sites, the sounds... but what ties them together?"

As they debated, a library assistant approached, her steps soft against the marble floor. She was a petite woman, her hair the silver-gray of well-read pages, her glasses perched precariously on the bridge of her nose.

"Excuse me, I couldn't help overhearing. You're tracking historical locations? Might I suggest cross-referencing with the city archives?" she offered, her voice a whisper honed by years of library service.

"Thank you, we might just do that," Vale replied, tipping an imaginary hat. "You wouldn't happen to have a tape player as well, would you?"

With a knowing smile, she nodded. "Follow me, detectives of history."

They trailed behind her to a room that smelled of dust and ink. Here, nestled between shelves laden with records, was a tape player, its buttons worn from use.

Eva inserted the first tape and pressed play. Harrow's voice filled the space, a spectral presence among the archives. They listened, pausing the playback occasionally to debate a sound or a reference.

"Did you hear that?" Michael interrupted, rewinding the tape. "That siren in the background—it's old, like from the forties or fifties. They don't make that sound anymore."

Eva's eyes lit up. "Of course! Harrow was telling us when. These tapes aren't just where, they're when. He's pinpointing an event in time."

The library assistant beamed, pleased with her part in their deduction. "I do enjoy a good mystery. Be sure to let me know how this chapter ends."

As they matched dates to the historical records, a timeline began to form—a series of incidents, long forgotten by the city, but all too relevant to their investigation.

"Guys, look at this!" Jenny exclaimed, pointing to an old newspaper clipping. "A heist from the fifties, unsolved. The description of the suspect... it matches 'The Shadow's' M.O."

Vale leaned over her shoulder, his face serious. "He's been operating for decades. Harrow must've uncovered his identity, but needed irrefutable proof."

"The kind of proof that you don't take to the cops because you don't know who's in on it," Michael muttered.

Eva gathered the tapes. "We need to go to these locations, find what Harrow left behind. It's the only way to bring 'The Shadow' into the light."

They packed up their clues, the library's silence a stark contrast to the urgency of their mission. As they stepped back into the sunlight, the city greeted them with the chaos of midday, indifferent to the drama unfolding in its midst.

Their next stop was a historical building in Lower Manhattan. Its facade was a patchwork of repair and neglect, the ghosts of the city's past etched into its very bricks.

Here, they found the echo of the siren from the tape, a hidden compartment that held another piece of the puzzle—a photograph, decades old, depicting a man shaking hands with a city official. The man's face was obscured, but the handshake spoke of deals and power.

"That's our connection," Vale said grimly. "'The Shadow' isn't just a criminal; he's part of the city's fabric. Harrow knew exposing him would shake the city to its core."

As they continued their journey from one historical site to the next, the city seemed to watch, its skyscrapers like sentinels over their progress. Each location held a key, each key unlocked a secret, and with each secret, the silhouette of 'The Shadow' grew ever more defined.

By the time the sun began to dip toward the horizon, painting the sky in hues of fire and gold, they had amassed enough evidence to piece together a story of corruption and silence that had haunted the city for generations.

As the day closed, they knew what lay ahead. Confrontation, revelation, and the risk that comes with dragging shadows into the unforgiving light of truth. But together, they had become the bearers of Harrow's legacy, the tellers of the final chapter of a story.

Eva, Vale, Jenny, and Michael gathered in the dim light of the evening at a round table strewn with the remnants of their investigation: the tapes, the manuscript, and now, a photograph they had unearthed from the depths of the city's archives.

"Harrow's clues have been leading us to places, yes, but more importantly, to moments—moments where 'The Shadow' felt invincible," Eva began, her finger tracing a circle around the date on the photograph. "Each location tied to a historic crime that had gone cold, unsolved."

Vale, his eyes hardened by years on the force, added, "The M.O. is consistent with our current string of crimes—the clever evasion, the almost theatrical setups, and the signature left behind. Harrow had seen this pattern before."

Jenny, ever the connector of dots, chimed in, "The timeline matches up. These aren't random acts; they're a history of manipulation. Look." She spread out the photos in a line. "Every major policy change, every shift in power. 'The Shadow' was there, an unseen hand tipping the scales."

"And always one step ahead," Michael interjected, his face serious. "Because he wasn't just hiding in the system; he was part of it. Someone with access to the inner workings of power. That's how he stayed untouchable."

A quiet understanding settled over the group. Harrow's manuscript wasn't just a retelling of his cases—it was a map of corruption, leading to a man whose influence was as broad as it was shadowy.

"The Morse code—it wasn't just a timestamp or a location identifier. It was Harrow's way of telling us when 'The Shadow' struck. Each code corresponds to a date, a crime that went unsolved, but not unnoticed," Eva said, a new gravity to her words.

"The manuscript—the allegories aren't just stories. They're parallels to the crimes, veiled descriptions of 'The Shadow's' methods," Vale added, his tone resolute.

The final piece clicked when they compared the dates of the crimes to public appearances and alibis of prominent figures, cross-referencing with Harrow's personal notes, discreetly acquired from his private study.

"One name kept showing up, a common thread through all these years," Eva said, holding up the photograph. "And in this picture, 'The Shadow' shakes hands with the mayor. But he's more than just a man in the crowd. He's someone we've all trusted."

Their eyes were drawn to the figure in the photo, a man whose face was turned away, his identity obscured by time and shadow, but now exposed by their relentless pursuit of truth.

"Councilman Gerard Blackwood," Jenny breathed out the name they had all come to suspect. A man of influence, of charisma—a man who'd been at the precinct the day Harrow's death was announced, feigning shock and offering condolences.

Vale's hands formed into fists. "Blackwood. I knew he was ambitious, but this... This is monstrous."

They knew now. Harrow had pieced it together, but he'd needed proof that would stand up against a man who had the city wrapped around his finger—a man who Harrow had suspected, but couldn't accuse without being silenced.

"He was silenced," Michael said, the realization cold and bitter.

But they had Harrow's message now, his legacy—a call to bring 'The Shadow' into the light.

They gathered their evidence, their resolve steeling them for the confrontation ahead. The night air was cool as they stepped out, a contrast to the fire that burned within them.

"We end this tonight," Eva said. "For Harrow, for the city, for justice."

The team moved out, the city's rhythm now a heartbeat pushing them forward towards an inevitable showdown. They had the truth; now they needed the world to hear it. The stage was set, the players in motion, and the final act of "The Last Manuscript" was about to be written.

10

The Final Reckoning

As dawn crept over the city, painting the sky with strokes of pink and gold, Eva, Jenny, Michael, and Detective Vale approached the grand, dilapidated manor that had once belonged to Councilman Gerard Blackwood. The manor stood like a sentry at the city's edge, its glory days long past, now cloaked in an aura of neglect and secrets.

"You sure this is the place?" Michael asked, his voice betraying a hint of doubt amidst the morning chorus of birds.

Vale, his face a mask of stoicism, nodded. "This is where Harrow's trail leads. Blackwood's ancestral home."

The manor's gates creaked open at their approach, the sound a mournful groan that seemed to echo with the weight of the untold stories held within its walls. The garden was a wild tangle of overgrowth, nature reclaiming its dominion.

Jenny adjusted the strap of her camera bag, her usual vibrancy tempered by the gravity of their mission. "Looks like the Addams family traded up," she quipped, trying to lighten the mood.

A chill breeze whispered through the trees, carrying with it the last remnants of night's chill. Eva wrapped her coat tighter around her as they made their way up the stone path.

"It's now or never," she said, her resolve steeling her against the unease that the house's imposing façade inspired.

They entered the main hall, their footsteps echoing off the marble floors and vaulted ceilings. Portraits of the Blackwood lineage stared down at them, eyes following their every move—a silent jury to the day's proceedings.

As they set up their makeshift command center on an ornate, dust-covered table, Vale's radio crackled to life, a reminder that they were not alone in their quest.

"We've got units in position. When you give the word, we move in," came the voice of Captain Reid, static-laced but clear.

Eva nodded to Vale, then turned to the others. "Once we present our evidence, there's no turning back. Blackwood will know we're onto him."

Michael, fiddling with the tape player, let out a nervous chuckle. "Here's to hoping he's a gracious loser."

They began to play the tapes, the voices from the past filling the room, detailing the web of corruption that Blackwood had woven throughout his career.

It wasn't long before the clatter of footsteps heralded the arrival of Blackwood himself, his demeanor one of arrogant disbelief.

"Detective Vale, to what do I owe the...pleasure?" Blackwood's voice was smooth, but the slight quiver betrayed his unease.

Eva stood to meet him, the evidence laid bare on the table before them. "Councilman Blackwood, we have proof of your involvement in numerous crimes over the years. It's over."

Blackwood's laugh was hollow, devoid of humor. "Do you think this charade will hold up? I have the city in my pocket."

Jenny stepped forward, a fire in her eyes. "Not anymore. The city's waking up, and so are its people."

The mood was electric, charged with the anticipation of justice long deferred. Blackwood's façade began to crack, the reality of his situation dawning on him.

As he realized the gravity of his predicament, the front door burst open, and Captain Reid entered, flanked by officers. "Gerard Blackwood, you are under arrest," he declared, the weight of the law behind his words.

The sun, now fully risen, cast beams of light through the stained glass windows, painting the scene in hues of redemption. Blackwood, the shadow that had loomed over the city, was now just a man in handcuffs.

Eva looked around at her team, their faces a mix of relief and exhaustion. They had done it; they had finished what Harrow had started.

Outside, the city stirred, its rhythm a bit more hopeful as the news began to spread. The shadow that had fallen over it for so long was finally lifting.

And in the heart of the city, in the homes and the streets, the story of 'The Last Manuscript' would be told and retold, a tale of truth's triumph over shadows, a reminder that even when darkness seems insurmountable, the light of justice can still prevail.